Coco's B

Tips for getting throug...

By Dr. Stephanie Liu, MD and Georgia Miller, MEd
Illustrated by Georgia Miller, MEd

COCO'S BAD DAY
Copyright © Stephanie Liu, 2021

All rights reserved. No part of this publication may be reproduced, stored in a retrieval system, or transmitted in any form or by any means, electronic, mechanical, photocopying, recording, or otherwise, without written permission of the author and publisher.

Published by Stephanie Liu, Edmonton, Canada

ISBN
Softcover   978-1-77354-336-9
Hardcover   978-1-77354-337-6

Publication assistance and digital printing in Canada by

PUBLISHING
PageMaster.ca

To all of the parents and children who have had bad days.

This book was created with love and care for you and your family to learn together and enjoy. We share strategies that we use with our own children.

Warmly,
Stephanie and Georgia

Coco had a bad day. Nothing seemed to go her way.

It all started when Coco's mom tried to get Coco to wear a hat.

"I will NOT wear this hat," whined Coco as she threw her hat across the room.

Coco's mother replied, "I understand you are not happy about wearing this hat. It is very hot today, so if you want to play at the park, you will need to put on your hat. Why don't we cuddle for a moment and then you can put it on?"

Coco thought about what her mother was saying. She knew her hat would protect her from the sun and after a few moments, Coco got up, grabbed her hat and put it on her head.

"I'm ready to go to the park!" beamed Coco.

Once Coco and her mother got to the park, Coco's mom took out a bottle of sunscreen.

Coco yelled, "NO SUNSCREEN!" and began to cry.

Coco's mom took a deep breath and looked at Coco. "Would you like to help me put sunscreen on both of us?"

Coco looked up at her mother and smiled. She put her paws out excitedly and helped apply the sunscreen.

When Coco got to her favorite slide, she noticed another puppy was using it. Coco waited and waited for her turn, but the puppy would not go down the slide!

"GET OFF!" Coco yelled and she pushed the puppy down the slide.

Coco's mother saw Coco push the puppy and
came over to make sure he was alright. Calmly,
Coco and her mother walked to the park bench to
talk.

"Coco, I will not allow you to push others because it hurts them. I'm not mad at you. I'm here to help you make safe choices because I love and care about you," said her mother.

Coco understood what her mother was saying.
She knew she should say sorry to the puppy.

Once they got home, Coco's mom made lunch. She was very tired from a hard morning with Coco.

When Coco sat down and saw her lunch she blurted out, "YUCK!" and threw her entire bowl on the floor.

Coco's mother was mad!

"COCO! I HAVE HAD ENOUGH! LOOK AT THIS MESS YOU MADE!"

Coco felt scared. She had made her mom very angry.

Mama didn't mean to scare Coco and always taught Coco not to yell at others.

"Coco," said mama, "I am sorry for yelling at you. I'm not perfect but I try my best."

Coco gave her a hug and said, "it's okay mama."

Coco's mother took a deep breath and said, "we are going to do a calming activity together."

They both sat down. Coco's mom crossed her arms across her chest, closed her eyes and began to tap her paws on each shoulder. Left then right, over and over again.

"Butterfly Hug" Inspired by Lucina Artigas and Ignacio Jarero

What are you doing mama? Coco asked

I am imagining my favorite place in the whole world while tapping my shoulders as a way to calm my body and mind.

Coco started to do the same.

"Butterfly Hug" inspired by Lucina Artigas and Ignacio Jarero

After a few minutes, they both felt much better. They got up and cleaned the mess off the floor.

Then it was time for Coco's nap.

Coco's mom cuddled up to Coco. "Tell me how you are feeling."

Coco looked up at her mother. "Sometimes I feel like I'm a bad puppy."

Coco's mom had tears in her eyes. "Coco, you're loved just the way you are and all puppies need a little help sometimes. That doesn't mean you're bad or that I will ever stop loving you."

Coco felt happy and had a nice long nap.

Meanwhile, Coco's mom had a warm bubble bath, her way of getting ready to do it all over again.

About the Author

Dr. Stephanie Liu is a family physician and Assistant Clinical Professor at the University of Alberta. She graduated from Columbia University with a Master of Science and completed her Doctor of Medicine at the University of Alberta. Dr. Liu is the creator of the evidence based parenting blog "Life of Doctor Mom." Her goal is to provide parents with accessible and credible medical information. She is also the founder of "By Dr. Mom," a company that creates functional and educational children's products. Outside of her work, Dr. Liu loves spending time with her husband Graeme and their two children, Madi and George.

 @lifeofdrmom www.lifeofdrmom.com
@bydrmom www.bydrmom.com

About the Author and Illustrator

Georgia is a teacher with Edmonton Public Schools and has a Masters in Elementary Education with a specialization in literacy and mental health. She completed her training at the University of Alberta and Harvard University. She also studied art in Italy and has a minor in Fine Arts. Georgia's life passion is giving unconditional support to children with mental health challenges. Most of all, Georgia loves being with her husband, Aaron and daughter, Tilly.

@mindfulbygeorgia